THE UNIVERSE ATE MY HOMEWORK

For my parents
—D.Z.

For my sister
—A.L.R.

Text copyright © 2018 by David Zeltser
Illustrations copyright © 2018 by Ayesha L. Rubio

Carolrhoda Books
A division of Lerner Publishing Group, Inc.
241 First Avenue North
Minneapolis, MN 55401 USA

For reading levels and more information, look up this title at www.lernerbooks.com.

Designed by Danielle Carnito.
Main body text set in Conduit ITC Std 18/21. Typeface provided by International Typeface Corp.
The illustrations in this book were created with Photoshop using digital drawing techniques.

Library of Congress Cataloging-in-Publication Data

Names: Zeltser, David, author.
Title: The universe ate my homework / David Zeltser; illustrated by Ayesha L. Rubio.
Description: Minneapolis : Carolrhoda Books, [2017] | Summary: "Abby really doesn't want to do her homework. So she creates a black hole to swallow it up . . . but the black hole turns into a baby universe!" —Provided by publisher.
Identifiers: LCCN 2016008148 (print) | LCCN 2016033621 (ebook) | ISBN 9781512430035 (eb pdf) | ISBN 9781512417982 (lb : alk. paper)
Subjects: | CYAC: Homework—Fiction. | Universe—Fiction.
Classification: LCC PZ7.Z3985 (ebook) | LCC PZ7.Z3985 Un 2017 (print) | DDC [E]—dc23

LC record available at https://lccn.loc.gov/2016008148

Manufactured in the United States of America
1-41144-23156-1/16/2018

THE UNIVERSE ATE MY HOMEWORK

DAVID ZELTSER

ILLUSTRATED BY AYESHA L. RUBIO

Carolrhoda Books • Minneapolis

Abby froze. Her least favorite thing in the whole wide universe was homework. She and Comet had WAY better things to do.

Like stargazing!

They settled into their secret spot just
as the first star was coming out.

"Abby?"

Ugh! Mom was closer than she thought!
Abby snuck around the house toward her dad.

"What are you thinking about, Dad?" she asked. He was a physicist and always puzzling about something or other.

"Our universe," he said.

"*Our* universe? Wait, do you mean there are *other* universes?"

Her dad's eyes twinkled like stars. "I think so! I've actually been working on some ideas for how to make a baby universe." He kissed her forehead. "Now, don't you have some homework to do?"

Abby's eyes lit up. "Yep! And I know just where to do it."

She kept reading.

You will need to squeeze so hard that the atoms in your object get very, very close to one another. So close that the atoms' gravity will take over and smash them together. This will create an invisible object called a mini black hole. Its gravity is so strong that it will pull in anything that gets too close. It is invisible because even light can't escape it.

"Abby," came her mother's voice, "are you doing your homework?"

"I've got it in my hands, Mom!" Abby didn't totally understand about the atoms, but she understood about the squeezing. She squeezed with all her might.

Even harder than she squeezed her mom's hand during thunderstorms.

POP! Her homework had become a black hole!

Abby peered in awe at the empty space where her homework had just been.

$$R_{\mu\nu} - \frac{1}{2} R g_{\mu\nu} + \Lambda g_{\mu\nu} = \frac{8\pi G}{c^4} T_{\mu\nu}$$

$$S = \frac{\pi A k c^3}{2 h G}$$

BZZZZZZZ went a nearby fly.

"Okay, Comet. Next step. To make a universe, we need to add energy!" She began to jump up and down.

$$R_{\mu\nu} - \frac{1}{2}R g_{\mu\nu} + \Lambda g_{\mu\nu} = \frac{8\pi G}{c^4} T_{\mu\nu}$$

$$S = \frac{\pi A k c^3}{2 h G}$$

BZZZZZZZ went a nearby fly.

FWOOP went the black hole, sucking the fly in.

$$R_{\mu\nu} - \frac{1}{2} R g_{\mu\nu} + \Lambda g_{\mu\nu} = \frac{8\pi G}{c^4} T_{\mu\nu}$$

$$S = \frac{\pi A k c^3}{2 \hbar G}$$

Comet nosed forward to investigate. His ears began to stretch. It was the black hole's gravity! He yelped as Abby yanked him back by his tail.

"Okay, Comet. Next step. To make a universe, we need to add energy!" She began to jump up and down.

Comet wagged his tail furiously.

Suddenly Abby could see something new forming. It was no longer pulling things into it. The black hole had turned into a baby universe. At first, Abby's universe was just a little bubbling broth of energy.

"Keep wagging, Comet!" she cried, turning cartwheels.

Her universe began to expand, and particles began to form. But it didn't push on anything as it expanded. Instead of taking up room, it somehow seemed to be creating its own space.

"Faster, Comet!"

As her universe grew, the particles clumped together and made bigger clouds of gas.

The clouds began to sparkle with explosions.

Stars were being born!

"ABBY, DID YOU FINISH YOUR HOMEWORK?"

She froze. It was her dad's voice outside the door. "Kind of," she replied.

Her father gazed in wonder. "You *made* this?"

Abby smiled proudly. "Yep! And I was thinking about living in it for a while. No homework in there, right?"

"Probably not," said her dad. "The only problem is once you're in there, I don't know of any way out."

Abby looked at her dad. Then she looked at the baby universe.

Abby ran to her dad and hugged him tight. "I think I'll stay," she said.

As Abby and her mom gazed at the Milky Way,
Abby's dad spotted Comet wolfing down the cookies.
"I guess no universe is perfect," he said.

"Yeah," replied Abby.
"But they're all amazing."

Dear ms. Hinz, sorry I didn't turn in my homework. I'm pretty sure it's somewhere but I don't know where that is. Anyway here is exactly what happened.

thanks for your understanding.
Abby

ABBY, PLEASE SEE ME AFTER CLASS!

AUTHOR'S NOTE

The legendary physicist Stephen Hawking once said, "Fact is stranger than fiction, and nowhere is that more true than in the case of black holes." A black hole is an infinitely dense point surrounded by a region of space with such strong gravity that nothing can escape from it, not even light. We can only detect it by its gravitational pull on other objects in space.

There are three main types of black holes. A mini black hole can be smaller than an atom but have the weight of a mountain. A medium-sized black hole, better known as a stellar black hole, is formed when a huge old star eventually collapses under its own weight. It is about the size of a city. Finally, a supermassive black hole can weigh as much as billions of stars combined and is about the size of a solar system. There is one such beast at the center of our galaxy.

Although the story in this book is entirely made up, the science behind it is not. Here I have to thank the innovative journalist Robert Krulwich and his guest on the "DIY Universe" episode of the *Radiolab* podcast, the brilliant physicist Brian Greene. Hearing them talk about how one might create a mini black hole—and then a baby universe—inspired me to write this book. The illustrator and I did use some artistic license in showing you what the baby universe looked like. Physicists don't think we could ever see or feel another universe from inside our own. But we can *imagine* it creating its own parallel space and forever expanding, just like the universe we live in.

As much as we know about black holes and baby universes, there are still plenty of unanswered questions out there. Can a black hole act as a portal from our universe to another? It's a complete mystery—a thrilling puzzle for the next generation of scientists to solve.